Alice Weil is half American and half German. She grew up in Bogota, Colombia, and attended the German and the French school. She is fluent in four languages. She has three children and seven grandchildren.

In 1990, she was kidnapped in Colombia for 269 days. After regaining her freedom, she settled in Europe. Since then she has travelled the world and immersed herself in the spiritual teachings of India, which she lives by. Through them she has been able to live her Dharma or life's purpose by serving others. *Mother Nature and the Agent* is her third published book.

ALICE WEIL

MOTHER
Nature and the Agent

AUSTIN MACAULEY PUBLISHERS™
LONDON • CAMBRIDGE • NEW YORK • SHARJAH

I dedicate this work to Mother Nature.

Introduction

Once upon a time many years ago, the world was calm, happy and healthy. The planet we call Earth, or our home (and by 'our' I mean the human race) used to be in complete harmony. The animals had their space; we humans didn't interact with them, and they didn't interact with us. The ocean's water was pristine and clear. The dolphins enjoyed surfing the waves and further south, on the shores of South Georgia Island, the penguins and elephant seals called the shoreline their home after leaving the vast waters of the Southern Ocean to travel inland to mate. When a ship came by, the penguins would stand on the shoreline trying to figure out who those strange creatures were, coming to impose themselves onto their habitat.

In the Amazon forest, the giant trees hid the sunlight and the sky. By some miracle, the smaller trees and plants were able to catch a small ray of sunlight or position themselves in such a way that they received the light they needed for their growth and wellbeing. The animals delineated their territory and the birds flew on high. The animal kingdom was very much at peace and lacked for nothing. There was plenty of food and water with an abundant plant world, enough to sustain their livelihood.

The giant lotus, known as the Victoria Regia, whose
leaves were so large one could stand on them
and not get one's feet wet, decorated the natural
ponds that had been formed by the Amazon river
and its rivulets. There was a certain respect among
humans. In those days, there were only books to be
read and various games to be played. There were
hikes and picnics and parents still had time to talk
to their children. Meals were consumed at home
and, it must be said, only one parent went to work.
Those were the days when the seasons honoured
their name. Winters were cold and the temperatures
dropped so low, much snow was created. The
summers were warm, even hot, but in those days
no human being's death was caused by a heat
wave. Nature went through its cycles and so did the
human race.
No one in his or her right mind ever thought that
this status quo would someday change. But change
did come, at a rather slow pace. Television was
invented and with that came an opening into the
world. The small planes that could travel only short
distances without refuelling became larger, enabling
more passengers to travel, thus reducing the fare.
Cargo ships no longer carried the freight in their
holds but were platforms on which huge containers
were placed. For centuries, humans have sailed
the various seas and oceans but suddenly, the
boating industry was soon creating bigger sailboats,
motorboats and yachts.

The culmination of this were the mega cruise ships that could carry thousands of passengers across the open seas. The ones who could afford these luxurious travels bragged about them to their friends and family; nobody who had the means wanted to be left behind. The automobile industry advanced as well. Cars were developed that could be driven at very high speeds; the only hitch was the amount of fuel they consumed. But that was not a problem; there was plenty of oil around, it was just a matter of price.

Yes, those were the days of plenty, not only in travel but in the construction world as well. The sky was the limit. Houses were knocked down to give way to buildings and those soon gave way to taller and taller ones; sometimes blocking out the sunlight for those who had gardens or balconies. Nobody cared. Those were the days of plenty, of power; the glory days of those who were financially well-off or could borrow money. Gone were the days when you had to work long hours and be creative in order to earn a good salary. The days in which even if one had a work schedule, the motto was, "Work Before Pleasure" and no one thought anything about putting in longer hours to get the job done. Those were the days when one had to save to be able to afford a house, or even a car. Those were the days, as I mentioned before, when harmony prevailed on Planet Earth.

But as things began to change in the world of mortals, things began to change on the planet, for the planet and its inhabitants are intimately connected. We humans tend to ignore this connection, but the connection does not ignore the actions we humans undertake.

As humans became more prosperous, and more and more people were able to afford luxury items such as meat, bigger houses, larger cars and easier travel (due to the opening of the borders where visas were no longer required to visit a country), Planet Earth began to suffer. And suffer it did. And although Planet Earth did not have a voice, it had an ally: Mother Nature. And while Mother Nature began to change, humans were blind, or simply didn't care. With the expansion of the meat industry came the need for nice, grassy fields for the cattle to feed upon. What better place than the Amazon jungle! Who cared about the gigantic trees and the habitat of all its wildlife, not to mention the indigenous peoples. So easy, it seemed. The land was free to take. Chop down the trees, turn the land into wonderful grazing pastures. More heads of cattle, more meat, more money, more luxury. Forgotten was the knowledge that the Amazon is Planet Earth's lungs. You might even say that it is the human race's extended lungs. Those trees that looked so useless, that were only 'taking up space', actually removed vast amounts of the CO_2 that we created in exchange for wonderful oxygen.

Prosperity began spreading far and wide. Every human on the planet wanted to be wealthy. Not only with their desire to travel, but to improve their quality of life as well. No matter if one had to sacrifice time spent with their children or the rest of the family, having two salaries to live on was far more important than bringing up and educating the offspring. Kids were left to fend for themselves. Gone were the days of family meals and home cooking. The appearance of fast food and takeaways, which also gave way to drive-throughs, were welcomed. Nature's produce was no longer good enough. The vegetables were too small in size and their shapes imperfect, thus giving rise to the GMO culture. The same held true for meat and poultry. Antibiotics and hormones were used to pump up the animals and, therefore, production. Somewhere along the way, we humans forgot that we are what we eat. Our bodies absorb what we take in. Our compassion and empathy towards nature was declining fast and compassion towards the animal kingdom began to fade as mass production continued to increase. With expanding richness within various societies, our increasing inflated ego, love and compassion were pushed aside. It slowly became all about me. Humans were no longer a part of the planet. Quite the contrary, the planet revolved around them. Mother Nature looked on in dismay at how everything was going in disarray.

The blue of the sky gave way to a greyish colour as more and more planes flew to different destinations, and nobody ever thought of reducing the number of flights. The more the merrier. The cities were hidden by a cloud of pollution, so thick that it was sometimes impossible to see through it. Yet more and more cars hit the road almost every day. Nobody cared. Mother Nature kept a vigilant eye out but did nothing – at first.We humans just kept our act going. More money, more prestige, more and more it was all about me. Then came the drugs and with them the addictions, sought after to replace the emptiness felt by the loneliness caused by lack of attention and caring. The values of friendships and family were relegated to second or third place. The money sign and career promotions had taken their place. So much prosperity brought a change in eating habits. Fast and fatty foods brought with them an increase in cholesterol and heart disease. Diabetes was on the rise, as was obesity. Clothing sizes that used to go from extra small, small, medium and large, were soon increased to X large and XXX. People's weight soon began to get out of hand; not only with adults but with children as well. It created uneasiness among some, giving rise to healthy foods stores which only appealed to a few. One day, Mother Nature decided she could no longer stand by and watch how Planet Earth was slowly deteriorating and decided to give us some warnings.

Chapter 1

Due to the amount of pollution, more and more humans were suffering from respiratory diseases such as bronchitis and asthma. The unstable weather was to blame for these illnesses – according to the doctors. However, a select few mentioned the real cause, but no one was willing to sacrifice the economic prosperity countries and people were experiencing in exchange for better air quality. The same held true for the increase in other medical issues. Cancer, heart disease, diabetes, they steadily rose, but here again, no one cared. "It's all part of the times we're living in" was the excuse.

WWII had ended 75 years before; the post war generations only knew a world of abundance, a world of unlimited consumption... if one had the pocketbook to pay for it.

The planet and Mother Nature were taken for granted. There was no time or interest in watching a sunset or a full moon, there were more enticing ways to spend one's time.

Mother Nature tried to make herself heard above the chatter and clatter, but only the scientists took notice. They warned about the glaciers decreasing in size. Of course, these effects went unnoticed except by the skiers, who watched with dismay with every passing winter the glaciers retreating more and more. The scientists warned of the ice cap becoming thinner and thinner in Greenland, about the temperatures rising in the Antarctica, but very few listened. Life went on as usual. Then the seasons began to change. There was less snowfall, less rain. The summer temperatures rose, giving way to heatwaves that set an end to a few people's lives. Nobody cared. Everyone noticed and commented but nothing actually happened.

Then Mother Nature decided to implement some really drastic measures. Unexpected tornadoes and cyclones swept through different parts of the planet, causing flooding, landslides and panic. The hurricane season came early, surprising everyone, not only with its intensity but frequency. Some people took notice and made a few comments but yet again, nothing changed. Something had to give. Storms brought with them very high winds and one sometimes wondered how the planes could keep on flying with such turbulence. The passengers held on for dear life; there was silence in the cabins, and everyone breathed a sigh of relief when either the turbulence stopped, or the captain landed the plane safely.

In some parts of the planet, rain turned to hail the size of golf balls, breaking windshields and doing other damage, the only comment from some was, "Maybe it's climate change", while other parts of the planet were hit by severe drought. Food was scarce and people were going hungry, famine was no longer a threat, it had become a reality. International institutions helped by sending food and giving credits, but life on the planet continued as usual.

Then one day, something extraordinary happened.
The Amazon jungle caught fire and Mother Nature
was not the cause. Humans were to blame. Cattle
owners, enticed by the international price of meat,
decided to expand their ranches and lost no sleep
over the animal kingdom they were about to
extinguish. The public outcry was massive.
"Climate change and CO2 emissions will only
increase!" Monetary gains for the countries involved
were far more important than saving the natural
habitat that was, in their eyes, worthless. But after
a while, the protests were forgotten, the Amazon
continued to burn, and life went on as usual.
The fires were finally extinguished by the help of
humans and Mother Nature.

Other awful fires burned across the planet. Australia's wildfires were almost impossible to put out and they scorched and destroyed massive areas of the country. The animals tried to flee, but a great number of them were doomed to die. Humans worked hard to put them out, but strong winds sabotaged their efforts. Humans also worked hard to save the animals that had miraculously survived the devastation but came away with burns all over their bodies. The fires lasted for weeks and weeks as the world watched in horror. They were followed by downpours of rain, which indeed put out the fires, but created floods the likes of which no one had ever seen. It was not only Australia where the lands burned, but in California as well.

Sparing nothing, multimillion-dollar homes went up in flames. Some of the comments going around were... "The planet is protesting our behaviour. Something has got to change." But we humans are not willing to change and leave our comfort zones, even if we are aware that warnings are being sounded and can be seen.
One is not willing to give up the pleasures or riches that have become engrained in our lives and lifestyle for others.

Chapter 2

Mother Nature was becoming increasingly frustrated and angry. Her messages and warnings were not being heeded. Much to her regret, she decided that something drastic had to happen. She spent a great deal of time thinking about it, then creating what she thought might be the way to teach these humans a lesson and make them mend their ways. This was not developed overnight, however. She researched the animal and vegetable kingdom and found several ideas in both realms, but it was the one she found in the animal kingdom that satisfied all her conditions.

She first tested her creation on a few animals, and when she got the reaction she had anticipated, she decided that the time had come for the human trials to begin. The infectious Agent could now be released. Invisible to the bare eye, it was discharged into space and it wafted into the moving breeze.

Smaller than a speck of dust, it settled onto objects.
Mother Nature had outdone herself. The Agent she
created could not attack the human body on its
own, which meant that to introduce itself into the
body, it had to be helped. Who were its helpers?
Some of us would have never guessed. They were
human hands.
Mother Nature observed in silence and rejoiced at
her creation. When the Agent settled on a surface,
it was doomed to stay there, unable to move on
his own, as I had mentioned. A hand placed on the
surface where the Agent lay became its means of
transportation, even though its destination was
unbeknownst to it. Usually, the hand would make
contact with the person's mouth or nose, even
his eyes. These were the secret entry points Mother
Nature had chosen for the Agent's journey into the
human body.

It embedded itself into it without manifesting itself. As if by a prior agreement, the body did not immediately react to the intruder. The Agent took its time reaching its destination and as it travelled, it analysed the health of the different systems that make up the human body. Mother Nature had added something to it that we could well call a weapon. Her creation had not been born with it. It had come to her as a second thought. She never stopped observing human behaviour and, therefore, came to the conclusion that the treatment could not be the same for everyone. Some deserved a lighter punishment than others. Coming up with a way to achieve this had given mankind some extra time.

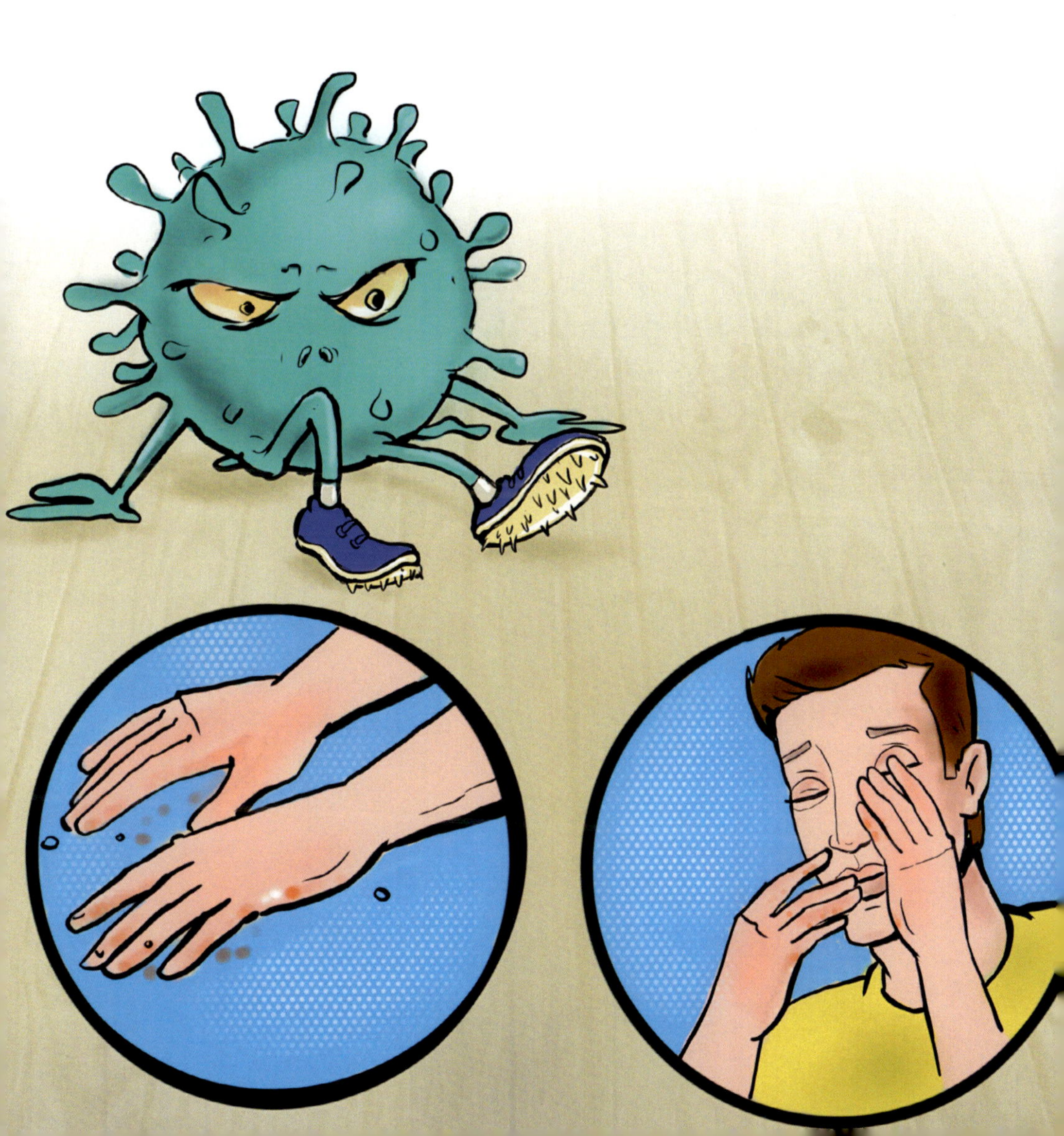

Once embedded in the body, it began to get acquainted with his surroundings. It was now an independent being and had the nourishment it required to thrive and grow. As it increased in size, the body began to send messages that something was wrong. The person felt unwell, had a temperature, showed signs of having a cold. He did not pay much attention to it and would tell a friend about his symptoms, saying, "It's just a cough and a runny nose, there's no reason for concern." And then a couple of weeks would go by and his friend would complain about the same things.

Much to Mother Nature's delight, the Agent was acting just as she had hoped; more and more people were feeling sick, but nobody could understand the reason or find out what was causing it. She had camouflaged the Agent so very well. It would take days, weeks and perhaps even years before humanity found out the real cause of the illness they were experiencing and develop a way to deal with it.

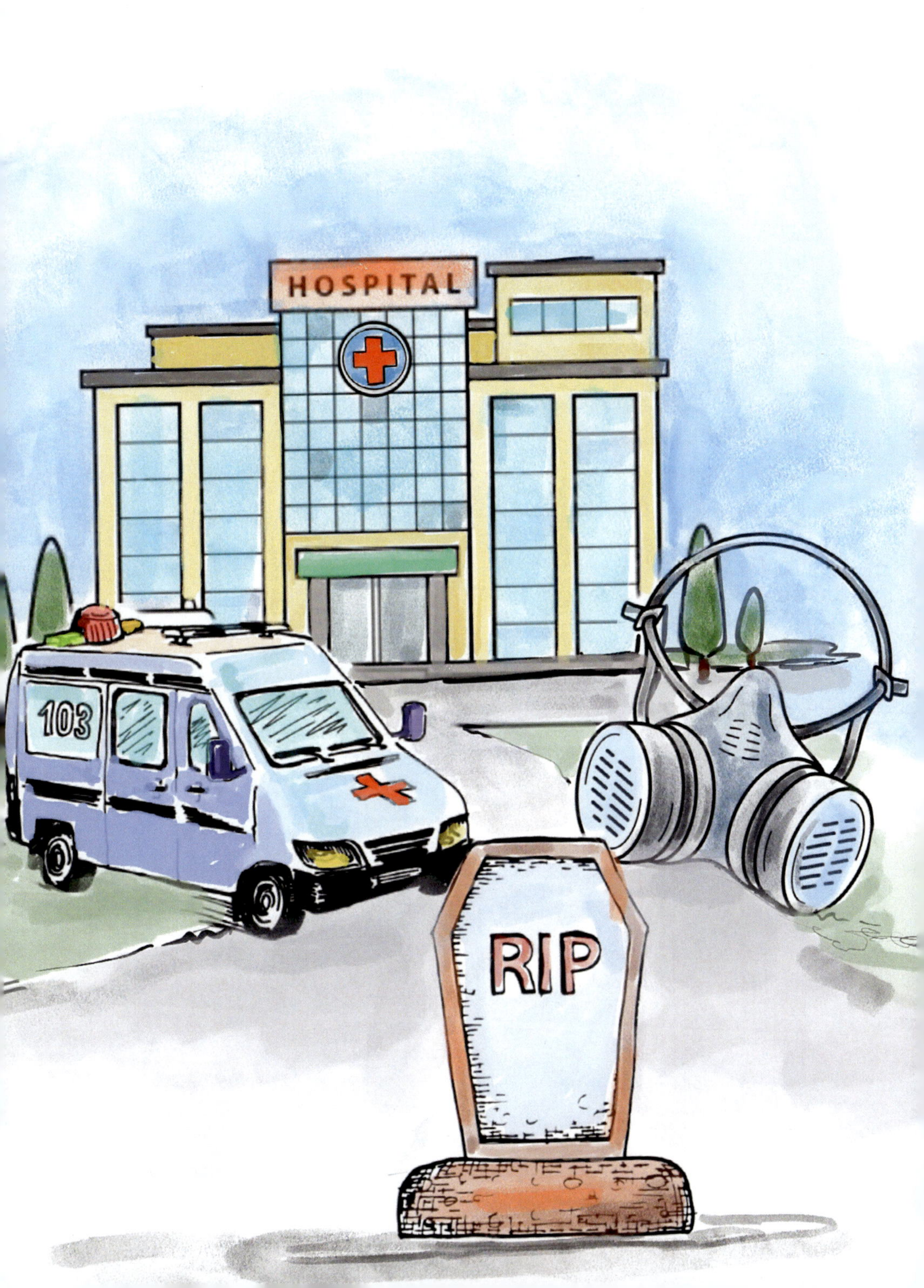

HOSPITAL
103
RIP

What made matters worse, no symptom was the
same. There was no consistency. The scientists
couldn't get a clear grasp of it. The Agent's
secret weapon was a set of spikes that could be
harmless or deadly, depending on where they
placed themselves, as well as the Agent's location
in the body. We could almost say they were
soldiers getting ready for battle. According to their
placement, they could be at the front causing
the worst damage by penetrating the lungs and
harming the tissue, causing the victim to struggle for
air and fight a battle doomed to lose from the start.

Placed in the midfield, they were worthless, and the person just developed flu or cold-like symptoms. Humanity was becoming more and more alarmed as time when on. Mother Nature had endowed the Agent with many different faculties. It could embed itself in the body and cause no damage and no sickness while at the same time implanting itself in another body. It hid in the droplets of a sneeze or a cough. It relied on the hands on which the droplets fell to touch the area of the mouth, nose or eyes, giving it access to the victim's body.

The Agent did not differentiate between age, race or sex. There were no limitations. It had free access. Mother Nature had also seen to it that the transmission could occur asymptomatically. Satisfied with her creation, she now sat back, relaxed and observed humanity's reaction.

Everyone was very much mystified when the disease first appeared. There was a lot of speculation as to what it might be as well as its cause. At first, it was said it was a disease that affected the respiratory track. Oxygen and ventilators were brought into the intensive care units. The number of sick people increased by the day. The disease spread like fire. It crossed from one continent to the other, from one country to another. They searched for a cure, but none was found. There was no inoculation against it, either. This was something completely unknown to mankind and the unknown unleashes fear and anguish. People did not understand what was happening to them. Some described it as having a cough or a little fever, others said it was just like having a cold. Some recovered very fast, others who felt they were recovering had a relapse and ended up in the intensive care units because they were suffering from shortage of breath.

Chapter 3

The mysterious disease appeared in Asia at first. People on other continents watched but paid little attention to what was happening. Asia and Africa had suffered from other strange diseases, but they had always remained there. What was happening seemed so far removed from the rest of the world and, of course, one must not forget, mankind has always soothed itself by saying: "This can't happen to me." We watched in amazement as a whole city was placed under lockdown mode. The number of people contracting the rare disease kept growing and so did the number of deaths. It was all over the news but, as I said before, there was no reason for concern, since it was happening there and had nothing to do with here.

How mistaken we were, how selfish of us. When the first cases arrived on our continent, we did not change our stance.

We continued to play the part of the untouchables. Some governments, and the World Health Organisation, had already started sounding some warnings, but by and large they went unheeded. The rate of contagion overwhelmed everyone. It was so unexpected. The words, "Wash your hands" or "Use disinfectant if you cannot wash your hands" and "Don't touch your face" were repeated day in / day out. The number of cases rose and so did the number of people who were dying in hospitals. One country closed its borders, only to be followed by the next one a couple of days
or weeks later.
We were afraid to speak to anyone for fear of being infected. In the meantime, the Agent enjoyed its fate, working its way soundlessly from one to the other. It was excellent in hiding its nature and changing its colour, just like a lizard does according to its whims. It could live in a body without manifesting itself whilst spreading its venom onto others. The mistrust between humans grew as they became aware of this factor. Shortly thereafter, quarantine orders were issued.

Confined
to the
HOME
A+

The population became a prisoner, not only in their countries but also in their own homes. The only activities allowed were to shop for groceries and a stop at the pharmacy. No one had ever lived through anything like it. Some worried about not having enough food and toilet paper. Little did they care about their neighbour. They filled their grocery carts until they couldn't fit one more item into them. It was the law of survival at its worst. I'll take what I need for myself, I don't care about the others. The stores were forced to ration products so that there was enough to go around. They warned over and over that the production and distribution lines were all up and running and there would be no disruption, yet it took a lot of time for people to realise this was indeed so.

Mother Nature stood by and watched the drama unfold. It brought out the very best and the very worse in the human being. It also brought out the best Mother Nature had to offer. With no more humans walking, moving and flying around, Mother Nature was able to recover from all the toxins we humans have filled the environment with. The noise level decreased considerably and all air travel, except cargo flights, were grounded. Without all that condensation, the sky showed us its true colour: dark blue. Air pollution disappeared and we were able to breathe in the vital energy force, prana in all its purity.

Animals ventured out into new surroundings. With
no humans around, the animals and birds were free
from fear and all boundaries had been lifted. They
felt unrestricted and went wherever, whenever.
Animals that had never ventured far from their
habitat were seen walking down Main Street.
The chirping of the birds and their songs were
louder than ever. Or was it because, with nowhere
to go and nothing to do, our awareness of the
environment had increased so much that it allowed
us to see and hear things that had gone unnoticed
before? Last but not least, the sunsets were
amazing, in vibrant colours and in such different
shades of red.

Each sunset more beautiful than the next. One could almost say they were competing, but with whom? Maybe the sun was just rejoicing at it being seen like the life-essential disc that had been worshipped by so many.
Locked up and not being able to go out, except for the mere essentials, our movements were reduced to pacing up and down in our own four walls. Those who had garden terraces and balconies could enjoy the outside. Those who did not were confined to going from one room to the next, or just staying in the only one they had. The confinement made us perhaps more aware of the have and have nots, one could almost say it showed the inequalities among us.

It also showed us how some were just happy and content at being able to occupy themselves with all those things they had always wished to do and were never afforded the time to do them. Others became anxious, restless and in some cases depressed. They were not used to being on their own, having to entertain themselves. We humans are able to adjust to all different circumstances; all it takes are a couple of days, maybe a couple of weeks. This time was no exception. Technology came to our aid; we were not cut off from the world. Yet the Agent continued to roam.

With our confinement, it had not disappeared. It was foremost on our minds; thinking, hearing and talking about it only brought out our fears. Watching the sunset, observing the night sky and admiring the stars, one could only wonder how such a peaceful and beautiful environment could be hosting such a deadly enemy that endangered us all. It lurked in the darkness, invisible to us all. The danger of it lodged within our bodies as we watched the number of deaths increase every day, making us suddenly aware of our mortality. We humans, who strongly believed the planet was ours and were meant to stay on it, suddenly realised that some force much more powerful than our ego and our arrogance could deal us a deadly blow within minutes.

It took just days for us to realise we had to change our lifestyle. Everything and everyone came to a complete standstill. All we had known until that day vanished before our eyes. Mother Nature gave us an unforgettable lesson in impermanence. This was nothing new, it had always been that way.

If one opens one's eyes and looks around at the
environment, one will notice that the blossom one
saw the day before is no longer there. We, too, are
impermanent, yet we are so self-centred that we
act as if our bodies were eternal. We do everything
to look young. Growing old is a sign of mortality, a
thought we want to avoid at all costs.
With the abrupt change in lifestyle, we suddenly
discovered our real essence: spiritual beings
at whose core lie love and compassion. It soon
became not about us but about others. The question
changed from "What I want" to "How can I help
and serve?" It was an amazing transformation.
Total strangers who had been neighbours for years,
never acknowledging their presence, were suddenly
speaking to one another. Total strangers joined
the neighbours in singing and dancing from their
balconies. It was truly amazing to see
how people interacted.
The streets were deserted as were the shops, except
for the essential ones.

Then, when we customers were told to keep our distance in the supermarket, no one spoke. We trusted no one, the thought on everyone's mind was: Be careful. We looked at each other, not with hate, nor love, but distrust. Home felt like a very safe place. It became our comfort zone. Some complained they had nothing to do and were bored, others looked at it as a time to relax and enjoy not being on a schedule. Some family bonds were strengthened, some parents got to know their children and enjoyed being able to spend that time with them. Others were not so happy.

The virus, however, was having its own troubles. With the confinement, it became an outcast. It could not spread since its mode of transportation had all but ceased. The number of people being infected began to diminish and so did the number of deaths. I do not know if Mother Nature really wanted it to be this way, or if we humans and our various governments had outwitted her. I believe the latter, since in those countries that refused to enforce the strict measures of confinement, the number of infected grew disproportionally day by day.

Chapter 4

Due to the reduction of the number of infected, countries began to open up their economies. It was a step-by-step procedure. Some people were allowed outside to exercise for a couple hours a day, some stores began to re-open. But it was not 'business as usual'. We celebrated these small acts of freedom with a great deal of misgiving. Hugs and kisses were banned and still are, social distancing has become ingrained in us. We do it almost automatically. The silence in the shops has not changed and we have become more confident in the knowledge that our enemy's territory has been reduced. With all the precautions taken, such as hand washing, social distancing and the wearing of masks, it was having a very difficult time spreading. But with time, we became more confident, less scared, thinking that we had the situation under our control.

However, we still keep reminding ourselves that we mustn't let our guard down. With no vaccine and no treatment, it's just waiting for another opportunity to continue invading and killing. It has succeeded in bringing out the injustice and unfairness that reign in this world. The poorest nations and its poorest people are the ones who have been hit the hardest. Those who cannot afford medical care, those who do not have a fixed income, and who have to take care of their livelihood every day, they have paid the price with their lives. It's so sad to watch. The ego-driven governments, for whom it is all about the people in power as opposed to the people who elected them, have turned their backs on their fellow citizens. People have come to realise that no empathy or compassion can be expected
from them.

Then something out of the ordinary happened. A white policeman murdered a black man. It was seen all over the world. Some passers-by filmed it and the video went viral. People from all over the world came together and mourned the life that had been taken. All of a sudden mankind realised that we are one humanity. Black life matters, white life matters, life matters, and the colour is irrelevant, we are humans, one race.

BLACK LIVES MATTER

Corona did not unite us, but the murder of a black man opened up our eyes to the fact that we are one. Our essence is love and compassion. Yes, we saw love and acts of compassion during the virus, but it took the murder of a black man to open our eyes to reality. We are one humanity. People went out to protest the killing and make their voices heard against police brutality in the US, forgetting all about the enemy that was hiding everywhere. Everyone let their guard down. Social distancing was forgotten, the rules of hand-washing and disinfectant were ignored. Mother Nature rejoiced. The obstacles to the Agent spreading had been removed. And spread it did. It was like a ball, bouncing from one to the next. People fell ill and were forced to stay at home, others were so sick they had to go to the hospital. The protest spread all over the world. Having recognised the oneness with all humanity, boundaries such as borders and frontiers had become non-existent. There was one cause, and it received worldwide attention.

Then, just when one thought the protest was becoming a thing of the past, another policeman killed a victim. This reignited the flame. The virus did not go away, it became stronger, it became more widespread, and it began to adapt easily to human culture. It's happy to be among us, creating havoc with our lives with anxiety and fear. It does not care. In the early stages, we were able to contain it by locking our doors, not socialising and changing our way of life. It had a hard time finding a way into our bodies. Now we have done its work for it by letting our guard down, by thinking we could go out as we used to and mingle with others, that no harm would come to us.

How mistaken we were. We have helped create a monster that grows day by day, one that has found the ways and means of surviving within us and among us. This will perhaps never change, or it might change when we realise that each one of us is responsible for the other. Our actions create reactions, which in this case means that by not observing the rules, we are creating the perfect environment in and around us, and it connects Corona to us all.

Some try to deny its very existence, living in a make-believe world in which everything is perfect. A return to the life we led before. But let us not be fooled. Sooner or later, we will be handed the bill for not having followed the advice and having believed in an illusion. We might also call it
wishful thinking.
Mother Nature has not been at all satisfied with the results of her creation. She has continued to beat the warning drum. Huge downpours followed by weeks on end without rain. Still we humans have not mended our ways. Some governments have chosen to ignore the obvious. Their scientific advisers have become non-existent. At one time, they took centre stage, giving almost daily advice and cautioning everyone about the dangers we faced. As the economic toll started to rear its head, as the numbers of unemployed became a liability to the interests of those who govern while thinking only of themselves and ignoring the people who have elected them, complacency set in. Masks and hygiene were forgotten. The number of infected and the dead rose again.

The containment that had been gained, was lost. There were more victims far and wide, the indifference was mind-boggling.

With summer on the doorstep, some countries were keen to open their borders in order to save the tourism industry on which so many countries are dependent. Some of us began to believe we were returning to some kind of normality. How wrong we were. The enemy reared its ugly head again, as some who returned had been careless by allowing the Agent in. It, in turn, was delighted. It could continue to wreak havoc – and that it did. It invaded others and pretty soon some were forced to quarantine yet again. We became aware once more that the enemy had not vanished.

We tend to forget about it, but when we hear or read about the mounting numbers of persons who are dealing with it, we are awoken from our dreamworld and are forced to confront reality. A reality that has, in a sense, robbed us of who we are. No hugs, no kisses, the wearing of masks has hidden our facial expressions. Our eyes reflect our emotions perhaps partially, but nothing can replace a grin or a smile.

As I survey the creation, I sometimes wonder if Mother Nature did not overdo it. I wonder if her creation did not overpower her and she ended up creating an uncontrollable monster. Yes, a monster who has grown tentacles, with which it is able to affect different parts of the body.

As the number of people infected with the Agent diminished, the countries opened up and with the opening, everyone seemed to have lost their memory. A kind of amnesia came over us. Mass gatherings took place, to the delight of the virus. It rejoiced and had a feast, finding more and more victims. To them, it would appear as though they had slept through a nightmare and the Agent's existence has been completely forgotten. Two weeks later, however, they will be reminded of it when it comes into action. The number of deaths will increase, we will once more be reminded not only of our fragility but also of our mortality.

We might be one humanity, but at the same time, we have lost all trust in each other.

We keep our distance from each other and the

thought that he or she might infect us is always in our minds. We will not regain our freedom until we realise that the battle cannot be won by one country alone. The whole planet has to unite and become one, with just one goal in mind: To defeat this enemy so that we might all be free again.

I may be wrong and Mother Nature not only wanted to show us that we have to take better care of our planet, but wanted to teach us that by looking in the same direction, by becoming aware of the need of others, and sharing our knowledge with each other, can we strive for a better future. I cannot think of anything more gratifying than love and compassion being shared by the whole of humanity. Once we remove envy, power, greed and jealousy and begin to act from the level of the divine that is in each one of us, will we succeed in not only regaining our freedom, but creating a whole new way of life; one that reflects our respect for the planet and for all of creation. Spirit will have been restored, empowering us to take the necessary steps in order to deal with climate change, having recognised that the environment is our extended body.

We depend on it for the vital energy, prana, or life force. We depend on it for clean water to quench our thirst and on the soil for our nourishment. Mother Nature will have achieved her goal of returning the planet to its pristine state and we humans will have finally become aware that, although each one of us are a ripple in the sea, together we are one. We are the ocean.